Meet The Covias

by Carolanne Donaldson

ISBN: 978-0-578-76172-5   (pbk, 8.5"w x 11"h)

Illustrations: Carolanne Donaldson
Interior formatting: Creative Sky Studio

To: James, Owen and Forrest

It depends on where you're living,
It depends upon the day-
What we didn't know yet,
Was change was on the way.

To begin with, change was gentle,
slowly spreading through the lands.
Then life as we had known it changed,
and social gatherings were banned.

I'd like to say this story starts with
"Once upon a time, in a land so very far away…"
For that would nicely rhyme,

But this story started recently,
And spread throughout the world.
As one by one our lifestyles-
Out the window they were hurled.

The virus was in China,
Then popped out for New Year's Eve.
It traveled slowly around the world,
And didn't seem to want to leave.

After spending time in Europe,
which is nicer in the summer,
the virus stopped to see the Queen,
And then came here… Oh, what a bummer!

With planes and trains and cars for all,
We can travel far and wide.
But when the virus climbed on board,
There was nowhere left to hide.

It rode on boats, it road on bikes,
It jumped up on our clothes.
It cannot live outside of us,
So it sneaks in through our nose.

Now a virus is a parasite,
It can't live without a host.
It needs someone to crawl inside,
whom can carry it coast to coast.

Now once things started changing,
Not all of them were bad.
But there were many other things,
That were really very sad.

They put us all in "quarantine."
We stayed home day after day.
Let's think of all the things we liked,
and the parts we hope will stay.

Graduations
cancelled.

Families &
Friends missed.

CANCELLED
DELAYED
DELAYED
CANCELLED

Elderly
alone.

Weddings
postponed.

Restaurants
closed.

Vacations
changed.

We like the fact we stay at home
And eat around the table.
Your mum and dad can do that,
Although many were not able.

We gobble it all up and plan out our meals,
And nothing goes to waste.
When you can't go to the store,
It's surprising what you'll taste!

We are reading books, playing school,
and catching up with chores.
Once that's all done, mumsy runs around
re-bleaching all the floors.

When grown-ups cleaned up every room,
We found out how much we had.
It's funny when you realize,
All of quarantine isn't so bad.

There are people walking dogs outside
While cleaning up the trash.
I hope that is a trend that stays,
Not leaving in a flash.

There are people cleaning up their yards,
And dads out playing catch.
They may have banned all sports for now,
But the kids all call out "it's a match!"

It's also nice to have the time
To just reach out and talk,
To call a friend or loved one,
When you are on a walk.

Of course the grandparents miss you kids,
And it's strange not to play.
But they are grateful for facetime calls,
And will play another day.

It's also really nice to know
That every country is talking.
They are trying to come up with cures
While we are all home or walking.

The scientists are busy,
And excited because it's new.
Plus an added bonus,
If we stay home we won't catch the flu!

We are learning how to cough and sneeze,
And not touch our face.
But not going out when you are sick,
Should always be the case.

We are washing hands while singing songs.
But along with all the hype,
Soap and toilet paper can't be found,
Did some people never wipe?

Not everyone is lucky, though.
Many have to go outside.
Doctors, nurses, firemen, police,
All have no time to hide.

We thank the people for our food,
For the farmers on the land.
To the person at the grocery store
Who lends a helping hand.

Maybe Mother Earth just needs a rest,
And sent us all to stay inside.
While she cleans up her air and land,
Her oceans, rivers and tides.

We help by cleaning our own space,
Then take a look about-
The world will be so sparkly clean,
When we finally get out!

Stay safe, sweet ones, and wash your hands.
Just stay home and you'll be fine.
We'll have a massive party soon,
Just at a different time.

We'll remember the Pandemic,
We are part of history now.
It won't be long till we come out,
And you can take a bow!

Hugs and kisses waiting!

"Coronavirus" – James Kayler, age 5

Made in United States
Orlando, FL
07 September 2022

22132353R00015